rainbow

Annual 1987

£3.50

Contents

Copyright © MCMLXXXVI by
Thames Television Limited.
All rights reserved
throughout the world.
Published in Great Britain by
World International Publishing Limited,
An Egmont Company,
Egmont House, P.O. Box 111, Great Ducie Street,
Manchester M60 3BL.
Printed in Italy.
SBN 7235 6779 4

Zippy Can't Get to Sleep

Zippy can't get to sleep. No matter how hard he tries he just doesn't feel sleepy.

At last he calls out, "George!"

But George is fast asleep and dreaming of strawberry milkshakes.

"Bungle!" calls Zippy.

"Oh, what is it, Zippy?" yawns Bungle, who had been fast asleep too.

"I can't sleep, Bungle," says Zippy.

"Sometimes when I can't get to sleep I say the letters of the alphabet and this makes me feel so tired that I soon fall asleep," says Bungle.

"Thank you, Bungle. That seems like a good idea," replies Zippy. "Goodnight, Bungle."

"Goodnight, Zippy," says Bungle.

Soon Bungle is fast asleep

again.

Zippy sits up in bed and says to himself, "A is for apple, b is for biscuit, c is for cake . . . and custard . . . and cream . . . saying the alphabet is making me feel very hungry."

"Bungle," he calls.

"Oh, what is it now?" says Bungle, waking up from a lovely dream.

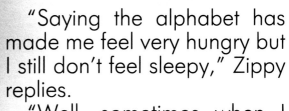

"Saying the alphabet has made me feel very hungry but I still don't feel sleepy," Zippy replies.

"Well, sometimes when I can't get to sleep I think of all the things that I will do the next day," says Bungle.

"Oh, yes, I never thought of that. Thank you, Bungle. Goodnight!" replies Zippy.

Soon Bungle is fast asleep once more.

Zippy thinks hard. "The first thing I will do tomorrow is have breakfast," Zippy says

to himself. "I will have a big glass of orange juice, a nice hot cup of tea . . . and lots of milk on my cereal . . . and thinking of all these things is making me feel very thirsty."

"Bungle!" he calls.

"Now what?" says Bungle, waking up again.

"Thinking of all the things that I will do tomorrow has made me feel very thirsty but I still don't feel sleepy," says Zippy.

"Then try counting to one hundred!" shouts Bungle.

Zippy tries this and by the time he reaches fifteen he is sound asleep. But now Bungle is wide awake! He says the letters of the alphabet forwards and backwards but he still doesn't feel sleepy. He thinks of all the things he is going to do tomorrow but he still doesn't feel sleepy. He counts to one hundred three times but he still doesn't feel sleepy!

Finally Bungle calls out, "George! What do you do when you can't get to sleep?"

A Picture Story

"What are you doing, George?" asks Bungle.

"I'm drawing a story," says George.

"Don't you mean *writing* a story?" asks Zippy.

"No, because I'm not writing. I'm drawing a picture story," says George.

"Can we see your picture story, please?" asks Geoffrey.

George shows them his first picture.

Zippy laughs. "It's a naughty little bear painting spots on his face!"

George shows them his second picture.

"Is this the little bear's mummy?" asks Bungle, pointing to the picture.

"Yes, it is," says George, "and when she sees the spots she thinks he is ill."

"Ha! ha! ha!" laughs Zippy.

George shows them his third picture. "In this picture they are going to see the doctor," explains George.

"Oh, no!" cries Zippy. "What happens next?"

"Well I haven't finished it yet," says George.

"Oh, do hurry up and finish it," says Zippy. "I want to know how it ends!"

So George goes off to finish his story.

Geoffrey has an idea. "We could watch George's story on our own television," he says.

"But how can we do that?" asks Bungle.

"I'll show you!" says Geoffrey.

What they need

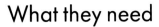

one large cardboard box
round-ended scissors
two long cardboard tubes
Sellotape
water paints

2. Bungle cuts two circles in one side of the box and two circles in the opposite side.

3. Zippy pushes the cardboard tubes through the holes.

What they do

1. Geoffrey cuts a big hole in the front of the box in the shape of a rectangle.

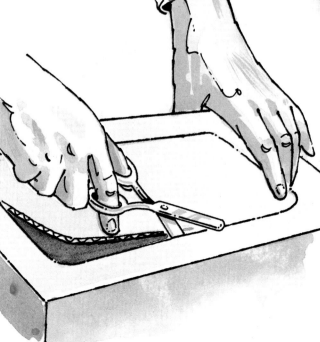

4. They paint the box a bright colour.

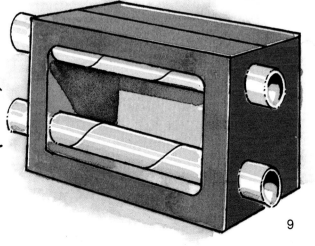

9

5. When George has finished his story Geoffrey puts the pictures in the right order, one below the other, and then Sellotapes them all together.

6. Next, he Sellotapes the beginning of the story to the top tube and the end of the story to the bottom tube.

7. George slowly turns the top tube and the pictures move up. It looks like a real television!

"There was once a little bear called Ben," George begins his story. "One day naughty Ben paints some spots on his face. His mummy sees the spots and thinks he is ill, so off they go to see the doctor. But on the way it starts to rain. Little bear's spots are washed away! Mummy bear is cross and she takes little bear home."

"Well done, George," says Geoffrey. "That was a good story."

"I thought it was very funny!" laughs Zippy.

"I thought so too," says Bungle. "I enjoyed it very much."

Why don't you make a picture story and show it to your friends on your own television, just like George did!

Making Clocks

Bungle, George and Zippy are going to a party. They are very excited, especially Zippy.

"When is Jane's party?" asks Zippy.

"It's at 4 o'clock this afternoon," says Bungle.

"I think I will get ready now then," replies Zippy.

"But it's only 1 o'clock, Zippy!" says Bungle. "It's much too early to get ready. There's lots of time yet. We will start to get ready at 3 o'clock. That's early enough."

"But how will we know when it's 3 o'clock?" asks George.

"I will tell you when it's 3 o'clock!" says Bungle.

replies Zippy. "Then we will be late."

"I won't forget, Zippy," says Bungle.

"Bungle," says Zippy. "If you show *me* how to tell the time on the clock then I will know when it's 3 o'clock and I will remind you if you forget!"

"Oh, all right then," says Bungle.

Bungle explains to Zippy that the numbers on the clock are the hours and that the little hand points to the number of hours that have gone past.

"At 3 o'clock the little hand points to three and the big hand points straight up," explains Bungle.

"But how will *you* know when it's 3 o'clock?" asks Zippy.

"I will look at the time on the clock!" says Bungle.

"But what if you forget?"

"Oh, yes. It's easy peasy!" says Zippy. "Now I will tell you when it's 3 o'clock, Bungle. You don't need to worry about forgetting anymore."

Zippy watches the clock for five minutes. The little hand doesn't seem to move at all and the big hand only moves very slowly. Soon, Zippy is bored.

"The hour hand isn't moving, Bungle," shouts Zippy. "I think this clock is broken."

"The clock isn't broken," says Bungle. "The hour hand is moving but it is moving so slowly that you can't see it."

"Well I'm fed up watching the clock," says Zippy. "Can I help you wrap Jane's present, please?"

"Yes, of course you can," says Bungle.

Bungle neatly wraps a square of pink paper round a big box of chocolates and Zippy sticks a big yellow bow on top.

"It looks very pretty," says George.

"Yes, it does," says Bungle. "Thank you for helping me, Zippy." But Zippy doesn't hear. He's wondering what to do next.

Zippy looks at the clock. It's not even 2 o'clock yet. He picks up one of his storybooks and starts to read. He looks at all the pictures and skips over all the hard words and soon he finishes the book.

"I think I will go to the library now," says Zippy. "I want to change this book."

"There's no time for that," says Bungle. "We will have to get ready for the party very shortly."

Zippy looks at the clock and he sees that the smaller hour hand is now pointing to the number 2. It's 2 o'clock.

"Why don't you make a clock?" says Bungle. "I'll show you how."

"Oh, yes. I'd like that!" says Zippy. "Then I will know all about time."

Bungle finds a small cardboard box and a round flat lid in their odds and ends drawer. He gets a piece of paper and, drawing round the lid, he makes a circle on the paper. He cuts out the circle with round-ended scissors. Bungle carefully writes the numbers of the hours inside the circle. He looks at the real clock to make sure that the numbers are in the right place. Next he cuts out a big hand and a little hand from a piece of cardboard. He

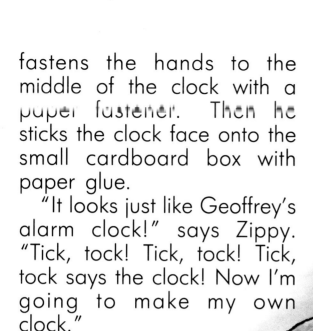

fastens the hands to the middle of the clock with a paper fastener. Then he sticks the clock face onto the small cardboard box with paper glue.

"It looks just like Geoffrey's alarm clock!" says Zippy. "Tick, tock! Tick, tock! Tick, tock says the clock! Now I'm going to make my own clock."

"Will you show me how to make a clock, Bungle?" asks George.

Bungle shows him how, and now each of them has a clock.

"Why don't we make a clock for Jane?" says Zippy.

"Yes. That's a good idea," says Bungle.

It's nearly 4 o'clock when at last Bungle notices the time on the real clock.

"Oh, no! We'll be late for the party!" he cries.

"And there will be no food left by the time we get there," says Zippy. "I knew you would forget, Bungle."

"But you forgot as well," says Bungle.

Geoffrey comes home from work and he is cross when he sees that they aren't ready for the party. But when Bungle tells Geoffrey why they are late for the party, he just laughs and isn't cross anymore.

"You were so busy learning all about time that in the end you forgot the time!" laughs Geoffrey.

Why don't you make a clock just like the one Bungle made in the story!

Day Time

Day Time

When it is light outside we say
it is day time.

Night Time

Night Time

When it is dark outside we say it is night time.

How is day time different from night time?

Finding Out About Time

A minute is a short time. Find out what you can do in one minute.

abcde

Can you say the alphabet in one minute?

Can you write your name in one minute?

Can you eat your breakfast in one minute?

An hour is a long time. Find out what you can do in one hour.

Can you have a bath in one hour?

Can you paint a picture in one hour?

Can you learn to read in one hour?

21

The Treasure Hunt

Bungle, George and Zippy are having lots of fun at Jane's party and after eating heaps of ice-cream and pink jelly, now it's time for the games.

"Who would like to go on a treasure hunt?" asks Jane.

"I would!" Zippy shouts loudly.

"Oh, yes please!" says Bungle.

"Wouldn't you like to go on a treasure hunt?" Jane asks George.

"I would rather stay here at the party and play games," answers George.

Jane laughs and explains to George that a treasure hunt is a party game.

"Oh, yes! Then I would like to very much!" he replies.

Jane explains the rules to everyone. "There are four

clues that will help you find the treasure. I am going to give you the first clue but you must find all the other clues yourselves." Jane gives Bungle a piece of paper. "This is the first clue," she says. "It's a sort of puzzle that you will have to think about very carefully."

"Oh, goody. I like puzzles!" says Zippy.

Bungle reads aloud the words of the first clue. "Look *at* something you usually look *through*!"

Bungle thinks hard about the words. George screws up his face into a frown, but Zippy thinks he knows the answer. "It's my sunglasses!

I look through them!" shouts Zippy. "But I haven't brought them with me."

"That's a *good* answer," says Jane. "But no, it's not the *right* answer, Zippy."

"It's the window!" shouts Bungle suddenly.

"Well done, Bungle," says Jane. "Yes, it is the window! Now, the clue says you look at something you usually look through."

"Then, we've got to look at the window," says Bungle.

George and Zippy rush

over to the window. "Here it is!" shouts George, holding up a small piece of paper. "I found it in the corner of the window."

George hands the second clue to Bungle, who reads it aloud. "Look *inside* something you usually wear *outside*!"

"I know!" shouts Bungle. "My hat. It's got to be my hat!" and he goes to get his hat from the stand in the hall. He looks inside it.

"Yes, it's there!" says Zippy, peering over his shoulder.

"That's only the label, silly," replies Bungle.

"Oh, no. I thought we'd found it then," says Zippy. "And now I've forgotten what the clue was."

So Bungle reads out the

clue again. "Look inside something you usually wear outside!"

"Then it's our shoes!" says Zippy.

"But how could Jane hide a clue inside our shoes when we've been wearing them all the time?" says Geoffrey. "I think the clue is in our coats."

"Yes!" they all shout together. Quickly they

search through their coats, and inside one of the big pockets in Bungle's coat is a small piece of paper. It's the third clue. Look for something *small* on something *tall*, it says.

"Good, this is an easy one," says Zippy. "Geoffrey is tall, the door is tall . . ."

"And the walls are tall," says George.

"Now we've got to look for something small on something tall," says Bungle. Then he notices a small picture on the wall and hidden behind it he can just see an edge of paper peeping out. It's the last clue.

"I've got it!" he shouts, taking the paper carefully from behind the picture. "It says, 'Look for something that's *square* under something that's *round*'."

"It's not fair," says Zippy. "This game is too difficult for me. I haven't worked out any of the clues, yet."

"Then you will have to think harder," says Geoffrey.

"But I can't think hard when I'm hungry," replies Zippy.

"Now, Zippy, you can't possibly be hungry. You've had at least six jellies," says Geoffrey.

"But there's still one left!" says Zippy. "Can I have that last one, please Geoffrey? Then I'll be able to think harder."

Geoffrey laughs. "All right, you can have that one jelly but nothing else," he says.

Zippy goes over to the party food laid out on the table and

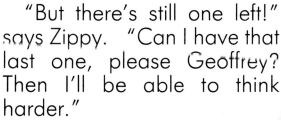

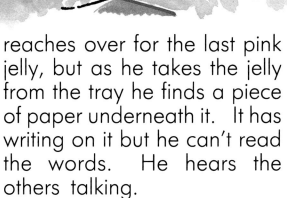

reaches over for the last pink jelly, but as he takes the jelly from the tray he finds a piece of paper underneath it. It has writing on it but he can't read the words. He hears the others talking.

"Something square," says Bungle, "under something that's round."

Zippy looks at the tray. It's square. He looks at the pink jelly. It's round. "I think I've

found the treasure!" he shouts.

Bungle takes the piece of paper from him and reads the words, "You have found the treasure!" written on it.

"Well done, Zippy," says Jane. "It was very clever of you to work out the answer all by yourself."

"It was easy peasy," says Zippy, and he smiles at Geoffrey. "But I thought we would win some *real* treasure, not just a jelly."

"But you have won some treasure!" says Jane, giving them each what looks like a bag of gold coins. "It's not *real* treasure, though."

Zippy takes off the gold paper from one of the chocolate coins. "I love chocolate money. It's better than *real* treasure!" laughs Zippy, and everyone agrees.

Animals Fly

This is George's favourite party game. It's lots of fun and it's very easy to play.

This is what you do

1. All players stand in a circle.
2. One person is chosen as the ringmaster.
3. The ringmaster stands in the middle of the circle and calls out something like "Eagles fly!" and everyone must flap their arms like wings.
4. But, if the ringmaster says "Hedgehogs fly!" then no one should wave their arms because hedgehogs cannot fly!
5. The game continues with the ringmaster calling out the names of different animals.
6. Any player who either forgets to wave their arms or waves their arms at the wrong time is out.
7 The last player left in the game is the winner. Why don't you try it yourself next time you have a party!

All Dressed Up!

Bungle, George and Zippy
like dressing up.
Can you guess what each of
them is pretending to be?

A Tat the Cat story . . .

by Audrey and Bill Titcombe

Having a Bad Time

Tat awoke to find the sun shining through the barn window. It's going to be a good day, he thought to himself. He stretched and quickly went out into the yard, where he found Oscar.

"Hello, Oscar!" said Tat cheerfully. "What a wonderful day it is."

"Hmmm. It might be for some," replied Oscar grumpily.

"What's the matter, Oscar?" asked Tat, concerned to see his friend looking so sad.

"Well," began Oscar, "the other day I buried a bone in a safe place and now I can't remember where I buried it. On top of that, the three posh ducks have just passed me on their way to the pond and they didn't say hello."

"Oh dear," said Tat. "You are having a bad time."

"Look," said Tat, "why don't we go for a nice walk in the woods. Perhaps that will cheer you up?"

"Well, if you think it will help," said Oscar.

So the two friends set off.

Once amongst the big trees and undergrowth, Oscar began to feel happier.

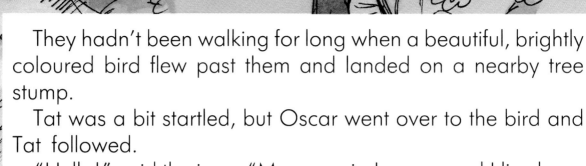

They hadn't been walking for long when a beautiful, brightly coloured bird flew past them and landed on a nearby tree stump.

Tat was a bit startled, but Oscar went over to the bird and Tat followed.

"Hello!" said the jay. "My name is Jeremy, and I live here. Can I help you?"

For a moment Tat was speechless, but then he found his voice and said, "Hello! My name is Tat and this is my friend Oscar. He is having a bad time today, so I thought a walk would cheer him up."

Jeremy turned to Oscar and said, "You haven't lost your bone by any chance, have you?"

"As a matter of fact," said Oscar, "I have."

"Well," said the jay. "I know exactly where it is. I saw you bury it in that little hollow a few days ago – follow me."

Oscar and Tat followed the bird.

Jeremy pointed with his beak to a hollow in the ground. "Try here," he said.

Using his big paws, Oscar started digging and within a few moments the bone appeared. Oscar was so pleased!

Oscar and Tat thanked Jeremy for his help and made their way home.

"You've not had such a bad time, after all!" said Tat to Oscar, once inside the barn. "You've found your bone and made a new friend. You should be very happy."

"I am!" said Oscar.

Can You Wink One Eye?

"Can you wink one eye?" Bungle asks George.

"Of course I can!" says George. "Look!" George looks into the mirror and blinks both eyes.

"Ha, ha, ha!" laughs Zippy. "You winked with both eyes, George."

Zippy tries next. He stops laughing when he sees that he can't wink, either.

Can *you* wink one eye?
Can you wink one eye and nod your head
at the same time?
Can you wink one eye, nod your head and
clap your hands at the same time?

"It's fun.   Try it yourself!" says Bungle.

ear
head
nose
eye
mouth
fingers
hand
chest
arm
leg
foot
toes

Find out what else
you can do
with your body.

Which Way to the Beach?

Bungle, George and Zippy want to find the shortest path to the beach.

How many steps has the red path?
How many steps has the blue path?
How many steps has the yellow path?
The shortest path has the smallest number of steps.
Which is the shortest path to the beach?

Bungle Sorts Things Out

Bungle, George and Zippy share the same bedroom. They have lots of things and they are not very tidy so sometimes their bedroom gets into a terrible mess. And today is one of those days. There are pencils in the paint box and racing cars in the laundry basket! There is a

shoe on the window sill and a vest in the odds and ends box!

"I really think we ought to tidy this room," says Bungle. "It looks very untidy."

"I agree. It does look untidy," says George. "Never mind, I will help you tidy up because much of this mess belongs to me."

"I don't see why I should help," says Zippy. "None of this mess is mine," and he picks up a book from the floor, sits on the bed and starts to read.

"I will collect all the clothes," says Bungle to George. "And you can collect all the toys."

Soon George has a big collection of toys.

"Shall we put everything away now?" asks George.

They find a shoe, a pair of pyjamas and a striped sock belonging to George. And inside George's sock they find one of Zippy's yellow slippers!

Zippy blushes an orange colour when they hand him his things.

"Oh, thank you," he says, and carries on reading his book.

"Now we will sort out the toys," says Bungle. "But let's sort them in a different way." Bungle thinks for a second.

"We've got to sort things out first," says Bungle. "Let's sort the clothes into three groups. We can put all my clothes in one group, all your clothes in a second group and all Zippy's clothes in a third group."

Bungle and George quickly sort out the clothes. They find a vest, two t-shirts, a pair of shorts and big sun hat belonging to Bungle. And inside Bungle's sun hat they find a pair of sunglasses belonging to Zippy!

"I know, why don't we put all the cars, trucks and things that we push along in one group?" says Bungle.

"Yes, that's a good idea," says George.

They find six cars, two trucks, one train and one robot with wheels for feet. "That makes ten things altogether," says George.

"Now let's put all the pencils and crayons in another group," says Bungle.

"What shall I do with this paint box and paper?" asks George.

"Well, why don't you put it with the pencils and crayons to make a group of things that we use for painting and drawing?"

"Yes. I'll do that," says George.

Soon they have four different groups. In the first group they have their push along things. In the second group they have things for painting and drawing. Can *you* remember what these things were? In the third group they have all their noisy toys. What do *you* think they put in this group? In the fourth group they have odds and ends—things like paper bags, empty boxes, buttons and bits of string.

George is putting away the

push along things when he finds a small, flat piece of wood in one of the trucks. He holds it up. "Look what I've found, Zippy!" shouts George.

Zippy knows what it is immediately. "It's part of the elephant's trunk!" he replies. "It's the piece that's missing from my animal jigsaw. I thought it was lost! Oh, thank you, George for finding it."

"And look what I've found," says Bungle. He holds up a small packet of sweets.

Zippy's eyes widen. "Where did you find those?" he asks.

"In this old box," says Bungle.

"But I thought I'd eaten them!" cries Zippy. "I'm sorry that I didn't help you both. Some of this mess was mine, after all."

"Well never mind," says Bungle. "Now that we've finished we can help you make your animal jigsaw."

"Oh yes, that would be fun! And you can share my sweets, too!" says Zippy, putting on his sunglasses and his yellow slippers.

Animal Groups

Bungle collects pictures of animals.
George is helping him sort out his animal pictures
into different groups.
This is the group Bungle made.

Why do you think Bungle put these
animals together in the same group?

This is the group George made.

Why do you think George put these animals together in the same group?
One of these animals could go in both groups.   Which one is it?

Answer: It's the fish. It can swim and it has stripes.

48

A Story That You Can Count

Look at the pictures, count the numbers out loud
and see if you can tell the story!

1 Count **one** rocket.

2 Count **two** stars.

3 Count **three** astronauts.

4 Count **four** clocks.

5 Count **five** planets.

6 Count **six** space creatures.

7 Count **seven** craters.

8 Count **eight** hills.

9 Count **nine** friends.

10

Count **ten** seconds.

Make a Bungle Puppet

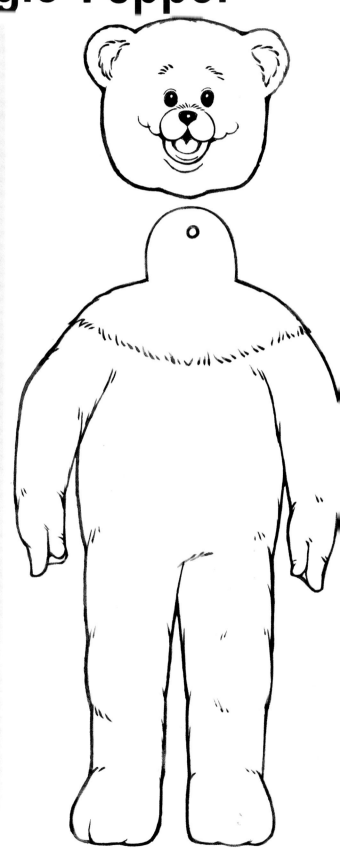

These instructions tell you how to make a moving puppet which looks just like Bungle. It's very easy but first you do need to ask a grown up to help.

What you need

two pieces of thin card
round-ended scissors
a paper fastener
two straws
Sellotape
crayons or felt pens

What you do

1. Draw the outline of Bungle's head onto thin card. You can copy or trace the drawings found on these pages if you want to.

2. Carefully cut out the shape of Bungle's head using round-ended scissors.

3. Next, draw the outline of Bungle's body onto the second piece of card and carefully cut it out.

4. Colour in Bungle's eyes, mouth and body using crayons or felt pens.

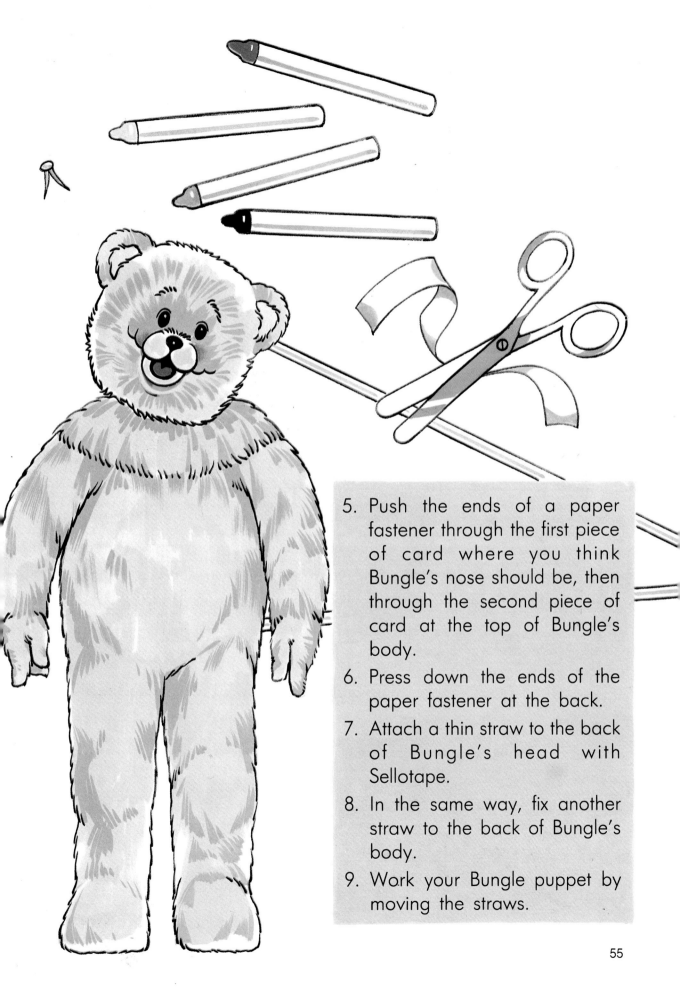

5. Push the ends of a paper fastener through the first piece of card where you think Bungle's nose should be, then through the second piece of card at the top of Bungle's body.

6. Press down the ends of the paper fastener at the back.

7. Attach a thin straw to the back of Bungle's head with Sellotape.

8. In the same way, fix another straw to the back of Bungle's body.

9. Work your Bungle puppet by moving the straws.

George
"Rainbow"

George Visits the Dentist

One day, George gets a letter in the post. He is very excited because he doesn't often get letters, except at Christmas and on his birthday.

"Who is it from?" asks Zippy, leaning over his shoulder.

The letter has lots of big words in it that George cannot read so Bungle reads the letter for him.

"It's from the dentist," says Bungle.

"Oh, that's nice," says George.

"What does it say?" asks Zippy.

"It tells George that it's time he went to see the dentist," replies Bungle.

"But I don't even have toothache!" says George.

"Then the letter must have come to the wrong house," says Zippy.

"But here is George's name written on the letter," says Bungle. "See for yourself," and he hands the letter to Zippy.

"Oh, yes!" says Zippy,

pretending he can read the words.

"The letter tells George that it's time he had a check-up of his teeth," says Bungle.

"But what's that?" asks Zippy.

"A check-up is what the dentist does when he checks our teeth," explains Bungle. "And it says here that you are to ring for an appointment."

"But I don't need any ointment!" replies George.

"Ha, ha, ha!" laughs Zippy. "Bungle said 'appointment' not 'any ointment'!"

"An appointment is the time when you can see the dentist," explains Bungle. "Now, when would you like an appointment?"

"I want an appointment straight after my breakfast!" replies George.

"Well, now we have to find out if the dentist can see you then," says Bungle. "Here is his telephone number."

Bungle slowly reads out the numbers and George dials each one on the telephone. Zippy presses his ear to the phone so that he too can hear it ringing. Soon it stops and a lady says, "Good morning!"

"Good morning!" reply George and Zippy together.

"I would like to make an appointment, please," says George.

"When would you like to come?" says the lady.

"Right now!" George replies, eagerly.

"The dentist is very busy this morning, George, and he can't see you right now but could you come at 3 o'clock this afternoon?" asks the lady.

"Oh, yes please!" replies George.

"Are we going to go with George?" whispers Zippy to Bungle

"Yes. We can't let him go alone, can we?" says Bungle. "He's too young to go by himself."

At 2 o'clock Bungle, George and Zippy leave the house. They are early for their appointment with the dentist and they have to sit in the waiting room.

Bungle reads the posters on the wall and Zippy looks at the pictures in the comics but

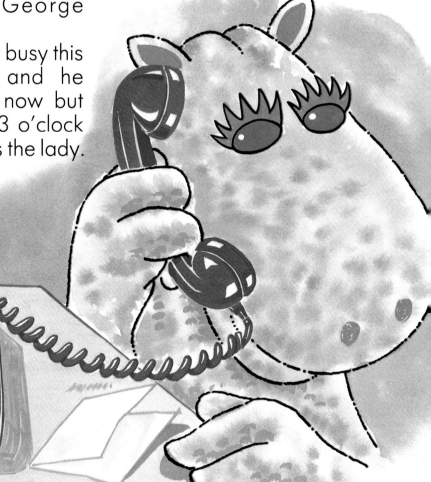

George just sits and waits. He looks very worried.

Soon it's 3 o'clock and George hears someone call his name. It's the lady he spoke to on the telephone.

Bungle and Zippy follow George into the surgery. That's the room where the dentist works.

"Good afternoon, George!" says the dentist. "Oh, I see you've brought your friends with you." The dentist says hello to Bungle and Zippy.

"We've only come to watch!" says Zippy.

George sits in a big chair. The dentist pulls down the back of the chair and looks into his mouth.

"He, he, he! Hasn't George got a big mouth?" says Zippy.

The dentist has a thin stick with a round mirror on the end

some second teeth too, you know."

"You must look after your second teeth," says the dentist, "because after these you don't get any more!"

"That's right," says Bungle. "We don't get third teeth, do we?"

Zippy doesn't look very happy when the dentist tells him that he mustn't eat too many sweets. "Too many sweets are not good for your teeth," he says. Then he gives them each a new

of it that he puts into George's mouth.

"What's that for?" whispers Zippy.

"It's so that the dentist can see the back of George's teeth," says Bungle.

The dentist doesn't find anything wrong with George's teeth and he tells him that two of his second teeth have started to grow. The dentist explains that his second teeth are his new teeth.

"Oh, I already know that," says Bungle. "Second teeth grow after first teeth. I have toothbrush and shows them how to brush their teeth properly.

"Round and round, a little bit at a time," they say together.

"I brush my teeth three times a day," says George.

"Well I brush mine eight times a day!" says Zippy.

"No you don't! That's a fib, Zippy!" says Bungle.

"Well, three times a day, after meals, is really quite enough, Zippy," the dentist tells him. "You don't want to

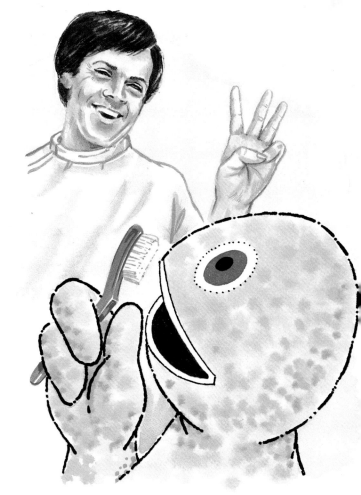

get toothache, do you?"

"I don't like having toothache," says George.

"Nobody does," says Bungle. "That is why we come for check-ups so that the dentist can make sure that we don't get toothache!"

"I am going to be a dentist when I grow up," says Zippy, "because now I know all about teeth!"

The dentist laughs and tells George to come back in six months time.

"But that's a long time," says George. "Can't I come again next week?"

Hide and Seek

George and Zippy are playing hide and seek in the park. Zippy has found a good hiding place and George can't find him. Can you help George find Zippy?

What you need

friends to play with
counters – a different one for
each player
a dice

How to Play

1. Throw the dice and move your counter forward the same number of squares as the number on the dice.
2. If you land on a picture square you must look at the chart to see what you have to do.
3. The winner is the first player to find Zippy!

 tree: go back two spaces

 flower: go forward two spaces

 toadstool: miss a throw

 squirrel: have another throw

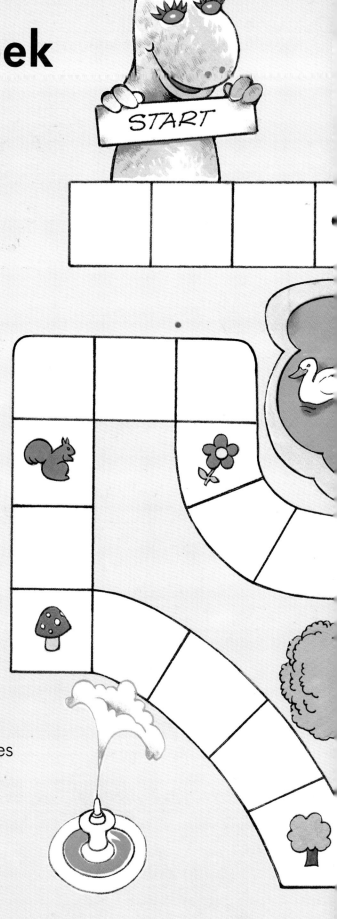